W9-AVK-348

This book belongs to

....

For my teachers who inspired me and the friends
and family who over the years have supported me.
You know who you are.

Goose Goes to School
Copyright © 2012 by Laura Wall
All rights reserved. Manufactured in China.

No part of this book may be used or reproduced in any manner whatsoever without
written permission except in the case of brief quotations embodied in critical articles
and reviews. For information address HarperCollins Children's Books, a division of
HarperCollins Publishers, 195 Broadway, New York, NY 10007.

www.harpercollinschildrens.com

ISBN 978-0-06-232437-5 (trade bdg.)

The artwork for this book was drawn with charcoal and finished digitally.

15 16 17 18 19   SCP   10 9 8 7 6 5 4 3 2 1

❖

First U.S. edition, 2015

Originally published in the U.K. by Award Publications Limited

Goose
GOES TO SCHOOL

by Laura Wall

HARPER
An Imprint of HarperCollinsPublishers

Today Sophie is going to school.

But Goose can't come.

Mom says geese aren't allowed in school.

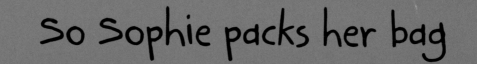

So Sophie packs her bag

and gets ready to go.

Sophie and Mom walk to school.

"Good-bye, Goose!"

But on the way to school, Sophie thinks

she hears flappy footsteps behind her.

And when she gets to the playground . . .

. . . she is sure she sees a familiar face.

But it can't be Goose, can it?

Mom said geese don't go to school.

Sophie goes into class

and finds her chair.

Sophie's first lesson is the alphabet.

She tries to listen, but she wishes Goose was with her.

But wait. What's that?

It can't be Goose. Can it?

It is Goose!

"Quick, Goose! Hide under the table."

The children start to giggle.

And the teacher gets mad.

But when she looks around,
she doesn't see Goose.

When the bell rings,
everyone runs outside to play.

Sophie and Goose play games.

Soon the other children want to
play with Sophie and Goose too.

Playtime is so much fun with Goose.

At the end of playtime . . .

. . . Sophie goes back to class.

And Goose flaps off to
play on the swings . . .

. . . and wait until school is over.

That afternoon everyone paints a picture.

The teacher loves their paintings.

She decorates the classroom wall with them.

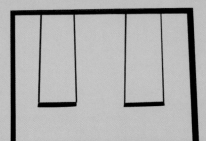

After school, Sophie waits for her mom

with her new friends.

They ask if Goose will be
back again tomorrow.

"What do you think, Goose?"

"Honk!" says Goose.